The stories at this level

These stories are fuller and a little more complex than those at Level 1. They introduce a greater number of characters, including all the residents of West Street. The words are repeated less frequently and the sentences are longer. At this level you should begin to emphasize the child's independent reading more.

Before you start reading with your children, read the story and activities first yourself, so that you become familiar with the text and the best way to give it expression and emphasis when reading it aloud.

Always sit comfortably with your child, so that both of you can see the book easily.

Read the story to your child, making it sound as interesting as possible. Add comments on the story and the pictures if you wish. Encourage your child to participate actively in the reading, to turn over the pages, and to become involved in the story and characters.

This may be enough for one sitting, but don't give your child the idea that the book is finished with. Encourage your child to take the book away and to look through it alone.

Next time you look at the book with your child, suggest "Let's read the story together. You join in with me." The text in the speech bubbles is often the same as the text at the bottom of the page, so one of you can read the text in the bubbles, and one can read the text at the bottom of the page. This time encourage your child to guess words from the context. Follow the words with your finger under them as you read. Don't stop to repeat words; keep the interest up and the story line flowing along.

Now ask your child, "Do you want to read the story to me this time?" If your child would like to do this, join in where necessary if help is needed.

The activities at this level

The activities at the back of the book need not be completed at once. They are not a test, but will help your child to remember the words and stories and to develop further the skills required for becoming a fluent reader.

The activities are often divided into three parts.

One part is designed to encourage you both to talk about the stories, and to link them where possible with your child's own experiences. Encourage your child to predict what will happen and to recall the main events of the story. Change the wording of the story as much as you like and encourage your children to tell you about the story in their own way.

One part encourages children to look back through the book to find general or specific things in the text or the pictures. Your child learns to begin to look at the text itself, and to recognise individual words and letters more precisely. The activities state clearly when you should give a letter its name, and when you should sound it out. The activities also introduce more writing, largely copying from words in the original story. If your children find this too difficult, copy the words onto a piece of paper for them to trace over.

One part suggests drawing or writing activities which will help your children feel they are contributing actively to the story in the book.

When you and your child have finished all the activities, read the story together again before you move on to another book. Your child should now feel secure with it and enjoy being able to read the story to you.

The big red bus

by Helen Arnold

Illustrated by Tony Kenyon

A Piccolo Original
In association with Macmillan Education

Here we are.

Hello, Mr Maggs.
Hello, Mrs Rocco.

5

Come on bus.

Is that the bus?

No. It's a car.

Hello, Mrs Rocco.
Is that the bus?

9

No. It's a lorry.

Is that the bus?

No. It's a motor-bike.

Is that the bus?

No. It's a van.

Where is the bus?

Come on bus.

It's coming.

Here comes the big red bus,

the big red bus,

the big red bus.

Here comes the big red bus

to take us to the shops.

One, please.

23

Thank you.

Two, please.

Thank you.

Here comes the big red bus,
The big red bus,
The big red bus.
Here comes the big red bus
To take us to the shops.

27

Things to talk about with your children

1. Do you remember who was in the bus queue?
Who was there first?
Who was there last?
How many of the people came from West Street?
Can you remember who all the people were?

2. Can your child write down the words on the bus stop without looking?
Talk about other street signs. How many can your child remember?

Looking at pictures and words
with your children

1. All these things came along the road. Can you point to them in the order they came along, without looking at the story?

Which came first?
Which came next?
Which came next?
Which came next?
Which came last?

Can you find the names of these things in the story?

2. Play 'I-Spy' with your child, using the picture above, for example:

"I spy with my little eye one of the things in the picture beginning with **m**. Can you tell me what it is?" (motor-bike)

At the end of the game, your child might like to take on the 'I-Spy' role.

Things for your child to do

1. Let's make up names for all the people at the bus stop who did not come from West Street.

2. Let's make a list of the people waiting for the bus.
You tell me who they are, and I'll write down their names.

Write the names on separate cards and later encourage your child to draw the people and match the names on the cards to the drawings.

3. Let's find the song that everybody sings when they get on the bus (page 27).
Shall we sing it together, following the words in the book?

Now try and see if you can sing it alone.

These activities and skills:	will help your children to:
Looking and remembering	hold a story in their heads, retell it in their own words.
Listening, being able to tell the difference between sounds	remember sounds in words and link spoken words with the words they see in print.
Naming things and using different words to explain or retell events	recognise different words in print, build their vocabulary and guess at the meaning of words.
Matching, seeing patterns, similarities and differences	recognise letters, see patterns within words, use the patterns to read 'new' words and split long words into syllables.
Knowing the grammatical patterns of spoken language	guess the word-order in reading.
Anticipating what is likely to happen next in a story	guess what the next sentence or event is likely to be about.
Colouring, getting control of pencils and pens, copying and spelling	produce their own writing, which will help them to understand the way English is written.
Understanding new experiences by linking them to what they already know	read with understanding and think about what they have read.
Understanding their own feelings and those of others	enjoy and respond to stories and identify with the characters.

First published 1989 by Pan Books Ltd,
Cavaye Place, London SW10 9PG

9 8 7 6 5 4 3 2 1

Editorial consultant: Donna Bailey

© Pan Books Ltd and Macmillan Publishers Ltd
1989. Text © Helen Arnold 1989

British Library Cataloguing in Publication Data
Arnold, Helen
The big red bus.
1. English language. Readers – For children
I. Title   II. Series
428.6
ISBN 0–330–30217–5

Printed in Hong Kong